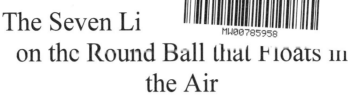
The Seven Li
on the Round Ball that Floats in
the Air

By
Jane Andrews

Coming Soon
How I Stole 5.6 Million from Walmart
The Gods Return Loki's Trial
Zombie Squirrels

Loki's Publishing

Seattle, WA

The Seven Little Sisters

Jane Andrew

Contents

The Seven Little Sisters

THE BALL ITSELF.

Dear children, I have heard of a wonderful ball, which floats in the sweet blue air, and has little soft white clouds about it, as it swims along.

There are many charming and astonishing things to be told of this ball, and some of them you shall hear.

In the first place, you must know that it is a very big ball; far bigger than the great soft ball, of bright colors, that little Charley plays with on the floor,—yes, indeed; and bigger than cousin Frank's largest football, that he brought home from college in the spring; bigger, too, than that fine round globe in the schoolroom, that Emma turns about so carefully, while she twists her bright face all into wrinkles as she searches for Afghanistan or the Bosphorus Straits. Long names, indeed; they sound quite grand from her little mouth, but they mean nothing to you and me now.

Let me tell you about *my* ball. It is so large that trees can grow on it; so large that cattle can graze, and wild beasts roam, upon it; so large that men and women can live on it, and little children too,—as you already know, if you have read the title-page of this book. In some places it is soft and green, like the long meadow between the hills, where the grass was so high last summer that we almost lost Marnie when she lay down to roll in it; in some parts it is covered with tall and thick forests, where you might wander like the "babes in the wood," nor ever find your way out; then, again, it is steep and rough, covered with great hills, much higher than that high one behind the schoolhouse,—so high that when you look up ever so far you can't see the tops of them; but in some parts there are no hills at all, and quiet little ponds of blue water, where the white water-lilies grow, and silvery fishes play among their long stems. Bell knows, for she has been among the lilies in a boat with papa.

Now, if we look on another side of the ball, we shall see no ponds, but something very dreary. I am afraid you won't like it. A great plain of sand,—sand like that on the seashore, only here there is no sea,—and the sand stretches away farther than you can see, on every side; there are no trees, and the sunshine beats down, almost burning whatever is beneath it.

Perhaps you think this would be a grand place to build sand-houses. One of the little sisters lives here; and, when you read of her, you will know what she thinks about it. Always the one who has tried it knows best.

Look at one more side of my ball, as it turns around. Jack Frost must have spent all his longest winter nights here, for see what a palace of ice he has built for himself. Brave men have gone to those lonely places, to come back and tell us about them; and, alas! some heroes have not returned, but have lain down there to perish of cold and hunger. Doesn't it look cold, the clear blue ice, almost as blue as the air? And look at the snow, drifts upon drifts, and the air filled with feathery flakes even now.

We won't look at this side longer, but we shall come back again to see Agoonack in her little sledge. Don't turn over yet to find the story; we shall come to it all in good time.

Now, what do you think of my ball, so white and cold, so soft and green, so quiet and blue, so dreary and rough, as it floats along in the sweet blue air, with the flocks of white clouds about it?

I will tell you one thing more. The wise men have said that this earth on which we live is nothing more nor less than just such a ball. Of this we shall know when we are older and wiser; but here is the little brown baby waiting for us.

The Seven Little Sisters

Jane Andrew

THE LITTLE BROWN BABY.

Far away in the warm country lives a little brown baby; she has a brown face, little brown hands and fingers, brown body, arms, and legs, and even her little toes are also brown.

And this baby wears no little frock nor apron, no little petticoat, nor even stockings and shoes,—nothing at all but a string of beads around her neck, as you wear your coral; for the sun shines very warmly there, and she needs no clothes to keep her from the cold.

Her hair is straight and black, hanging softly down each side of her small brown face; nothing at all like Bell's golden curls, or Marnie's sunny brown ones.

Would you like to know how she lives among the flowers and the birds?

She rolls in the long soft grass, where the gold-colored snakes are at play; she watches the young monkeys chattering and swinging among the trees, hung by the tail; she chases the splendid green parrots that fly among the trees; and she drinks the sweet milk of the cocoanut from a round cup made of its shell.

When night comes, the mother takes her baby and tosses her up into the little swinging bed in the tree, which her father made for her from the twisting vine that climbs among the branches. And the wind blows and rocks the little bed; and the mother sits at the foot of the tree singing a mild sweet song, and this brown baby falls asleep. Then the stars come out and peep through the leaves at her. The birds, too, are all asleep in the tree; the mother-bird spreading her wings over the young ones in the nest, and the father-bird sitting on a twig close by with his head under his wing. Even the chattering monkey has curled himself up for the night.

Soon the large round moon comes up. She, too, must look into the swinging bed, and shine upon the closed eyes of the little brown baby. She is very gentle, and sends her soft light among the branches and thick green leaves, kissing tenderly the small brown feet, and the crest on the head of the mother-bird, who opens one eye and looks quickly about to see if any harm is coming to the young ones. The bright little stars, too, twinkle down through the shadows to bless the sleeping child. All this while the wind blows and rocks the little bed, singing also a low song through the trees; for the brown mother has fallen asleep herself, and left the night-wind to take care of her baby.

So the night moves on, until, all at once, the rosy dawn breaks over the earth; the birds lift up their heads, and sing and sing; the great round sun springs up, and, shining into the tree, lifts the shut lids of the brown baby's eyes. She rolls over and falls into her mother's arms, who dips her into the pretty running brook for a bath, and rolls her in the grass to dry, and then she may play among the birds and flowers all day long; for they are like merry brothers and sisters to the happy child, and she plays with them on the bosom of the round earth, which seems to love them all like a mother.

This is the little brown baby. Do you love her? Do you think you would know her if you should meet her some day?

A funny little brown sister. Are all of them brown?

We will see, for here comes Agoonack and her sledge.

The Seven Little Sisters

Jane Andrew

AGOONACK, THE ESQUIMAU SISTER.

What is this odd-looking mound of stone? It looks like the great brick oven that used to be in our old kitchen, where, when I was a little girl, I saw the fine large loaves of bread and the pies and puddings pushed carefully in with a long, flat shovel, or drawn out with the same when the heat had browned them nicely.

Is this an oven standing out here alone in the snow?

You will laugh when I tell you that it is not an oven, but a house; and here lives little Agoonack.

Do you see that low opening, close to the ground? That is the door; but one must creep on hands and knees to enter. There is another smaller hole above the door: it is the window. It has no glass, as ours do; only a thin covering of something which Agoonack's father took from the inside of a seal, and her mother stretched over the window-hole, to keep out the cold and to let in a little light.

The Seven Little Sisters

Here lives our little girl; not as the brown baby does, among the trees and the flowers, but far up in the cold countries amid snow and ice.

If we look off now, over the ice, we shall see a funny little clumsy thing, running along as fast as its short, stout legs will permit, trying to keep up with its mother. You will hardly know it to be a little girl, but might rather call it a white bear's cub, it is so oddly dressed in the white, shaggy coat of the bear which its father killed last month. But this is really Agoonack; you can see her round, fat, greasy little face, if you throw back the white jumper-hood which covers her head. Shall I tell you what clothes she wears?

Not at all like yours, you will say; but, when one lives in cold countries, one must dress accordingly.

First, she has socks, soft and warm, but not knit of the white yarn with which mamma knits yours. Her mamma has sewed them from the skins of birds, with the soft down upon them to keep the small brown feet very warm. Over these come her moccasins of sealskin.

If you have been on the seashore, perhaps you know the seals that are sometimes seen swimming in the sea, holding up their brown heads, which look much like dogs' heads, wet and dripping.

The seals love best to live in the seas of the cold countries: here they are, huddled together on the sloping rocky shores, or swimming about under the ice, thousands and thousands of silver-gray coated creatures, gentle seal-mothers and brave fathers with all their pretty seal-babies. And here the Esquimaux (for that is the name by which we call these people of the cold countries) hunt them, eat them for dinner, and make warm clothes of their skins. So, as I told you, Agoonack has sealskin boots.

Next she wears leggings, or trousers, of white bear-skin, very rough and shaggy, and a little jacket or frock, called a jumper, of the same. This jumper has a hood, made like the little red riding-hoods which I dare say you have all seen. Pull the hood up over the short, black hair, letting it almost hide the fat, round face, and you have Agoonack dressed.

Is this her best dress, do you think?

Certainly it is her best, because she has no other, and when she goes into the house—but I think I won't tell you that yet, for there is something more to be seen outside.

Agoonack and her mother are coming home to dinner, but there is no sun shining on the snow to make it sparkle. It is dark like night, and the stars shine clear and steady like silver lamps in the sky, but far off, between the great icy peaks, strange lights are dancing, shooting long rosy flames far into the sky, or marching in troops as if each light had a life of its own, and all were marching together along the dark, quiet sky. Now they move slowly and solemnly, with no noise, and in regular, steady file; then they rush all together, flame into golden and rosy streamers, and mount far above the cold, icy mountain peaks that glitter in their light; we hear a sharp sound like Dsah! Dsah! and the ice glows with the warm color, and the splendor shines on the little white-hooded girl as she trots beside her mother.

It is far more beautiful than the fireworks on Fourth of July. Sometimes we see a little of it here, and we say there are northern lights, and we sit at the window watching all the evening to see them march and turn and flash; but in the cold countries they are far more brilliant than any we have seen.

[Illustration]

It is Agoonack's birthday, and there is a present for her before the door of the house. I will make you a picture of it. "It is a sled," you exclaim. Yes, a sled; but quite unlike yours. In the faraway cold countries no trees grow; so her father had no wood, and he took the bones of the walrus and the whale, bound them together with strips of sealskin, and he has built this pretty sled for his little daughter's birthday.

It has a back to lean against and hold by, for the child will go over some very rough places, and might easily fall from it. And then, you see, if she fell, it would be no easy matter to jump up again and climb back to her seat, for the little sled would have run away from her before she should have time to pick herself up. How could it run? Yes, that is the wonderful thing about it. When her father made the sled he said to himself, "By the time this is finished, the two little brown dogs will be old enough to draw it, and Agoonack shall have them; for she is a princess, the daughter of a great chief."

Now you can see that, with two such brisk little dogs as the brown puppies harnessed to the sled, Agoonack must keep her seat firmly, that she may not roll over into the snow and let the dogs run away with it.

You can imagine what gay frolics she has with her brother who runs at her side, or how she laughs and shouts to see him drive his bone ball with his bone bat or hockey, skimming it over the crusty snow.

Now we will creep into the low house with the child and her mother, and see how they live.

Outside it is very cold, colder than you have ever known it to be in the coldest winter's day; but inside it is warm, even very hot. And the first thing Agoonack and her mother do is to take off their clothes, for here it is as warm as the place where the brown baby lives, who needs no clothes.

It isn't the sunshine that makes it warm, for you remember I told you it was as dark as night. There is no furnace in the cellar; indeed, there is no cellar, neither is there a stove. But all this heat comes from a sort of lamp, with long wicks of moss and plenty of walrus fat to burn. It warms the small house, which has but one room, and over it the mother hangs a shallow dish in which she cooks soup; but most of the meat is eaten raw, cut into long strips, and eaten much as one might eat a stick of candy.

They have no bread, no crackers, no apples nor potatoes; nothing but meat, and sometimes the milk of the reindeer, for there are no cows in the far, cold northern countries. But the reindeer gives them a great deal: he is their horse as well as their cow; his skin and his flesh, his bones and horns, are useful when he is dead, and while he lives he is their kind, gentle, and patient friend.

The Seven Little Sisters

There is some one else in the hut when Agoonack comes home,—a little dark ball, rolled up on one corner of the stone platform which is built all around three sides of the house, serving for seats, beds, and table. This rolled-up ball unrolls itself, tumbles off the seat, and runs to meet them. It is Sipsu, the baby brother of Agoonack,—a round little boy, who rides sometimes, when the weather is not too cold, in the hood of his mother's jumper, hanging at her back, and peering out from his warm nestling-place over the long icy plain to watch for his father's return from the bear-hunt.

When the men come home dragging the great Nannook, as they call the bear, there is a merry feast. They crowd together in the hut, bringing in a great block of snow, which they put over the lamp-fire to melt into water; and then they cut long strips of bear's meat, and laugh and eat and sing, as they tell the long story of the hunt of Nannook, and the seals they have seen, and the foot-tracks of the reindeer they have met in the long valley.

Perhaps the day will come when pale, tired travellers will come to their sheltering home, and tell them wonderful stories, and share their warmth for a while, till they can gain strength to go on their journey again.

Perhaps while they are so merry there all together, a very great snowstorm will come and cover the little house, so that they cannot get out for several days. When the storm ends, they dig out the low doorway, and creep again into the starlight, and Agoonack slips into her warm clothes and runs out for Jack Frost to kiss her cheeks, and leave roses wherever his lips touch. If it is very cold indeed, she must stay in, or Jack Frost will give her no roses, but a cold, frosty bite.

This is the way Agoonack lives through the long darkness. But I have to tell you more of her in another chapter, and you will find it is not always dark in the cold northern countries.

HOW AGOONACK LIVES THROUGH THE LONG SUMMER.

It is almost noon one day when Agoonack's mother wraps the little girl in her shaggy clothes and climbs with her a high hill, promising a pleasant sight when they shall have reached the top.

It is the sun, the beautiful, bright, round sun, which shines and smiles at them for a minute, and then slips away again below the far, frozen water.

They haven't seen him for many months, and now they rejoice, for the next day he comes again and stays longer, and the next, and the next, and every day longer and longer, until at last he moves above them in one great, bright circle, and does not even go away at all at night. His warm rays melt the snow and awaken the few little hardy flowers that can grow in this short summer. The icy coat breaks away from the clear running water, and great flocks of birds with soft white plumage come, like a snowstorm of great feathery flakes, and settle among the black rocks along the seashore. Here they lay their eggs in the many safe little corners and shelves of the rock; and here they circle about in the sunshine, while the Esquimau boys make ready their long-handled nets and creep and climb out upon the ledges of rock, and, holding up the net as the birds fly by, catch a netful to carry home for supper.

The sun shines all day long, and all night long, too; and yet he can't melt all the highest snowdrifts, where the boys are playing bat-and-ball,—long bones for sticks, and an odd little round one for a ball.

It is a merry life they all live while the sunshine stays, for they know the long, dark winter is coming, when they can no longer climb among the birds, nor play ball among the drifts.

The seals swim by in the clear water, and the walrus and her young one are at play; and, best of all, the good reindeer has come, for the sun has uncovered the crisp moss upon which he feeds, and he is roaming through the valleys where it grows among the rocks.

The old men sit on the rocks in the sunshine, and laugh and sing, and tell long stories of the whale and the seal, and the great white whale that, many years ago, when Agoonack's father was a child, came swimming down from the far north, where they look for the northern lights, swimming and diving through the broken ice; and they watched her in wonder, and no one would throw a harpoon at this white lady of the Greenland seas, for her visit was a good omen, promising a mild winter.

Little Agoonack comes from her play to crouch among the rocky ledges and listen to the stories. She has no books; and, if she had, she couldn't read them. Neither could her father or mother read to her: their stories are told and sung, but never written. But she is a cheerful and contented little girl, and tries to help her dear friends; and sometimes she wonders a great while by herself about what the pale stranger told them.

And now, day by day, the sun is slipping away from them; gone for a few minutes to-day, to-morrow it will stay away a few more, until at last there are many hours of rosy twilight, and few, very few, of clear sunshine.

But the children are happy: they do not dread the winter, but they hope the tired travellers have reached their homes; and Agoonack wants, oh, so much! to see them and help them once more. The father will hunt again, and the mother will tend the lamp and keep the house warm; and, although they will have no sun, the moon and stars are bright, and they will see again the streamers of the great northern light.

Would you like to live in the cold countries, with their long darkness and long sunshine?

It is very cold, to be sure, but there are happy children there, and kind fathers and mothers, and the merriest sliding on the very best of ice and snow.

The Seven Little Sisters

Jane Andrew

GEMILA, THE CHILD OF THE DESERT.

It is almost sunset; and Abdel Hassan has come out to the door of his tent to enjoy the breeze, which is growing cooler after the day's terrible heat. The round, red sun hangs low over the sand; it will be gone in five minutes more. The tent-door is turned away from the sun, and Abdel Hassan sees only the rosy glow of its light on the hills in the distance which looked so purple all day. He sits very still, and his earnest eyes are fixed on those distant hills. He does not move or speak when the tent-door is again pushed aside, and his two children, Alee and Gemila, come out with their little mats and seat themselves also on the sand. You can see little Gemila in the picture. How glad they are of the long, cool shadows, and the tall, feathery palms! how pleasant to hear the camels drink, and to drink themselves at the deep well, when they have carried some fresh water in a cup to their silent father! He only sends up blue circles of smoke from his long pipe as he sits there, cross-legged, on a mat of rich carpet. He never sat in a chair, and, indeed, never saw one in his life. His chairs are mats; and his house is, as you have heard, a tent.

The Seven Little Sisters
Do you know what a tent is?

I always liked tents, and thought I should enjoy living in one; and when I was a little girl, on many a stormy day when we couldn't go to school, I played with my sisters at living in tents. We would take a small clothes-horse and tip it down upon its sides, half open; then, covering it with shawls, we crept in, and were happy enough for the rest of the afternoon. I tell you this, that you may also play tents some day, if you haven't already.

The tent of Gemila's father is, however, quite different from ours. Two or three long poles hold it up, and over them hangs a cloth made of goats'-hair, or sometimes sheepskins, which are thick enough to keep out either heat or cold. The ends of the cloth are fastened down by pegs driven into the sand, or the strong wind coming might blow the tent away. The tent-cloth pushes back like a curtain for the door. Inside, a white cloth stretched across divides this strange house into two rooms; one is for the men, the other for the women and children. In the tent there is no furniture like ours; nothing but mats, and low cushions called divans; not even a table from which to eat, nor a bed to sleep upon. But the mats and the shawls are very gorgeous and costly, and we are very proud when we can buy any like them for our parlors. And, by the way, I must tell you that these people have been asleep all through the heat of the day,—the time when you would have been coming home from school, eating your dinner, and going back to school again. They closed the tent-door to keep out the terrible blaze of the sun, stretched themselves on the mats, and slept until just now, when the night-wind began to come.

Now they can sit outside the tent and enjoy the evening, and the mother brings out dates and little hard cakes of bread, with plenty of butter made from goats' milk. The tall, dark servant-woman, with loose blue cotton dress and bare feet, milks a camel, and they all take their supper, or dinner perhaps I had better call it. They have no plates, nor do they sit together to eat. The father eats by himself: when he has finished, the mother and children take the dates and bread which he leaves. We could teach them better manners, we think; but they could teach us to be hospitable and courteous, and more polite to strangers than we are.

When all is finished, you see there are no dishes to be washed and put away.

The stars have come out, and from the great arch of the sky they look down on the broad sands, the lonely rocks, the palm-trees, and the tents. Oh, they are so bright, so steady, and so silent, in that great, lonely place, where no noise is heard! no sounds of people or of birds or animals, excepting the sleepy groaning of a camel, or the low song that little Alee is singing to his sister as they lie upon their backs on the sand, and watch the slow, grand movement of the stars that are always journeying towards the west.

Night is very beautiful in the desert; for this is the desert, where Abdel Hassan the Arab lives. His country is that part of our round ball where the yellow sands stretch farther than eye can see, and there are no wide rivers, no thick forests, and no snow-covered hills. The day is too bright and too hot, but the night he loves; it is his friend.

He falls asleep at last out under the stars, and, since he has been sleeping so long in the daytime, can well afford to be awake very early in the morning: so, while the stars still shine, and there is only one little yellow line of light in the east, he calls his wife, children, and servants, and in a few minutes all is bustle and preparation; for to-day they must take down the tent, and move, with all the camels and goats, many miles away. For the summer heat has nearly dried up the water of their little spring under the palm-trees, and the grass that grew there is also entirely gone; and one cannot live without water to drink, particularly in the desert, nor can the goats and camels live without grass.

Now, it would be a very bad thing for us, if some day all the water in our wells and springs and ponds should dry up, and all the grass on our pleasant pastures and hills should wither away.

What should we do? Should we have to pack all our clothes, our books, our furniture and food, and move away to some other place where there were both water and grass, and then build new houses? Oh, how much trouble it would give us! No doubt the children would think it great fun; but as they grew older they would have no pleasant home to remember, with all that makes "sweet home" so dear.

And now you will see how much better it is for Gemila's father than if he lived in a house. In a very few minutes the tent is taken down, the tent-poles are tied together, the covering is rolled up with the pegs and strings which fastened it, and it is all ready to put up again whenever they choose to stop. As there is no furniture to carry, the mats and cushions only are to be rolled together and tied; and now Achmet, the old servant, brings a tall yellow camel.

Did you ever see a camel? I hope you have some time seen a living one in a menagerie; but, if you haven't, perhaps you have seen a picture of the awkward-looking animal with a great hump upon his back, a long neck, and head thrust forward. A boy told me the other day, that, when the camel had been long without food, he ate his hump: he meant that the flesh and fat of the hump helped to nourish him when he had no food.

Achmet speaks to the camel, and he immediately kneels upon the sand, while the man loads him with the tent-poles and covering; after which he gets up, moves on a little way, to make room for another to come up, kneel, and be loaded with mats, cushions, and bags of dates.

Then comes a third; and while he kneels, another servant comes from the spring, bringing a great bag made of camels'-skin, and filled with water. Two of these bags are hung upon the camel, one on each side. This is the water for all these people to drink for four days, while they travel through a sandy, rocky country, where there are no springs or wells. I am afraid the water will not taste very fresh after it has been kept so long in leather bags; but they have nothing else to carry it in, and, besides, they are used to it, and don't mind the taste.

Here are smaller bags, made of goats'-skin, and filled with milk; and when all these things are arranged, which is soon done, they are ready to start, although it is still long before sunrise. The camels have been drinking at the spring, and have left only a little muddy water, like that in our street-gutters; but the goats must have this, or none at all.

The Seven Little Sisters

And now Abdel Hassan springs upon his beautiful black horse, that has such slender legs and swift feet, and places himself at the head of this long troop of men and women, camels and goats. The women are riding upon the camels, and so are the children; while the servants and camel-drivers walk barefooted over the yellow sand.

It would seem very strange to you to be perched up so high on a camel's back, but Gemila is quite accustomed to it. When she was very little, her mother often hung a basket beside her on the camel, and carried her baby in it; but now she is a great girl, full six years old, and when the camel kneels, and her mother takes her place, the child can spring on in front, with one hand upon the camel's rough hump, and ride safely and pleasantly hour after hour. Good, patient camels! God has fitted them exactly to be of the utmost help to the people in that desert country. Gemila for this often blesses and thanks Him whom she calls Allah.

All this morning they ride,—first in the bright starlight; but soon the stars become faint and dim in the stronger rosy light that is spreading over the whole sky, and suddenly the little girl sees stretching far before her the long shadow of the camels, and she knows that the sun is up, for we never see shadows when the sun is not up, unless it is by candlelight or moonlight. The shadows stretch out very far before them, for the sun is behind. When you are out walking very early in the morning, with the sun behind you, see how the shadow of even such a little girl as you will reach across the whole street; and you can imagine that such great creatures as camels would make even much longer shadows.

Gemila watches them, and sees, too, how the white patches of sand flush in the morning light; and she looks back where far behind are the tops of their palm-trees, like great tufted fans, standing dark against the yellow sky.

She is not sorry to leave that old home. She has had many homes already, young as she is, and will have many more as long as she lives. The whole desert is her home; it is very wide and large, and sometimes she lives in one part, sometimes in another.

As the sun gets higher, it begins to grow very hot. The father arranges the folds of his great white turban, a shawl with many folds, twisted round his head to keep off the oppressive heat. The servants put on their white fringed handkerchiefs, falling over the head and down upon the neck, and held in place by a little cord tied, round the head. It is not like a bonnet or hat, but one of the very best things to protect the desert travellers from the sun. The children, too, cover their heads in the same way, and Gemila no longer looks out to see what is passing: the sun is too bright; it would hurt her eyes and make her head ache. She shuts her eyes and falls half asleep, sitting there high upon the camel's back. But, if she could look out, there would be nothing to see but what she has seen many and many times before,—great plains of sand or pebbles, and sometimes high, bare rocks,—not a tree to be seen, and far off against the sky, the low purple hills. They move on in the heat, and are all silent. It is almost noon now, and Abdel Hassan stops, leaps from his horse, and strikes his spear into the ground. The camel-drivers stop, the camels stop and kneel, Gemila and Alee and their mother dismount. The servants build up again the tent which they took down in the morning; and, after drinking water from the leathern bags, the family are soon under its shelter, asleep on their mats, while the camels and servants have crept into the shadow of some rocks and lain down in the sand. The beautiful black horse is in the tent with his master; he is treated like a child, petted and fed by all the family, caressed and kissed by the children. Here they rest until the heat of the day is past; but before sunset they have eaten their dates and bread, loaded again the camels, and are moving, with the beautiful black horse and his rider at the head.

They ride until the stars are out, and after, but stop for a few hours' rest in the night, to begin the next day as they began this. Gemila still rides upon the camel, and I can easily understand that she prays to Allah with a full heart under the shining stars so clear and far, and that at the call to prayer in the early dawn her pretty little veiled head is bent in true love and worship. But I must tell you what she sees soon after sunrise on this second morning. Across the sand, a long way before them, something with very long legs is running, almost flying. She knows well what it is, for she has often seen them before, and she calls to one of the servants, "See, there is the ostrich!" and she claps her hands with delight.

The ostrich is a great bird, with very long legs and small wings; and as legs are to run with, and wings to fly with, of course he can run better than he can fly. But he spreads his short wings while running, and they are like little sails, and help him along quite wonderfully, so that he runs much faster than any horse can.

Although he runs so swiftly, he is sometimes caught in a very odd way.
I will tell you how.

He is a large bird, but he is a very silly one, and, when he is tired of running, he will hide his head in the sand, thinking that because he can see no one he can't be seen himself. Then the swift-footed Arab horses can overtake him, and the men can get his beautiful feathers, which you must have often seen, for ladies wear them in their bonnets.

All this about the ostrich. Don't forget it, my little girl: some time you may see one, and will be glad that you know what kind of a fellow he is.

The ostrich which Gemila sees is too far away to be caught; besides, it will not be best to turn aside from the track which is leading them to a new spring. But one of the men trots forward on his camel, looking to this side and to that as he rides; and at last our little girl, who is watching, sees his camel kneel, and sees him jump off and stoop in the sand. When they reach the place, they find a sort of great nest, hollowed a little in the sand, and in it are great eggs, almost as big as your head. The mother ostrich has left them there. She is not like other mother-birds, that sit upon the eggs to keep them warm; but she leaves them in the hot sand, and the sun keeps them warm, and by and by the little ostriches will begin to chip the shell, and creep out into the great world.

The ostrich eggs are good to eat. You eat your one egg for breakfast, but one of these big eggs will make breakfast for the whole family. And that is why Gemila clapped her hands when she saw the ostrich: she thought the men would find the nest, and have fresh eggs for a day or two.

This day passes like the last: they meet no one, not a single man or woman, and they move steadily on towards the sunset. In the morning again they are up and away under the starlight; and this day is a happy one for the children, and, indeed, for all.

The morning star is yet shining, low, large, and bright, when our watchful little girl's dark eyes can see a row of black dots on the sand,—so small you might think them nothing but flies; but Gemila knows better. They only look small because they are far away; they are really men and camels, and horses too, as she will soon see when they come nearer. A whole troop of them; as many as a hundred camels, loaded with great packages of cloths and shawls for turbans, carpets and rich spices, and the beautiful red and green morocco, of which, when I was a little girl, we sometimes had shoes made, but we see it oftener now on the covers of books.

All these things belong to the Sheik Hassein. He has been to the great cities to buy them, and now he is carrying them across the desert to sell again. He himself rides at the head of his company on a magnificent brown horse, and his dress is so grand and gay that it shines in the morning light quite splendidly. A great shawl with golden fringes is twisted about his head for a turban, and he wears, instead of a coat, a tunic broadly striped with crimson and yellow, while a loose-flowing scarlet robe falls from his shoulders. His face is dark, and his eyes keen and bright; only a little of his straight black hair hangs below the fringes of his turban, but his beard is long and dark, and he really looks very magnificent sitting upon his fine horse, in the full morning sunlight.

Abdel Hassan rides forward to meet him, and the children from behind watch with great delight.

Abdel Hassan takes the hand of the sheik, presses it to his lips and forehead, and says, "Peace be with you."

Do you see how different this is from the hand-shakings and "How-do-you-do's" of the gentlemen whom we know? Many grand compliments are offered from one to another, and they are very polite and respectful. Our manners would seem very poor beside theirs.

Then follows a long talk, and the smoking of pipes, while the servants make coffee, and serve it in little cups.

Hassein tells Abdel Hassan of the wells of fresh water which he left but one day's journey behind him, and he tells of the rich cities he has visited. Abdel Hassan gives him dates and salt in exchange for cloth for a turban, and a brown cotton dress for his little daughter.

It is not often that one meets men in the desert, and this day will long be remembered by the children.

The next night, before sunset, they can see the green feathery tops of the palm-trees before them. The palms have no branches, but only great clusters of fern-like leaves at the top of the tree, under which grow the sweet dates.

Near those palm-trees will be Gemila's home for a little while, for here they will find grass and a spring. The camels smell the water, and begin to trot fast; the goats leap along over the sand, and the barefooted men hasten to keep up with them.

In an hour more the tent is pitched under the palm-trees, and all have refreshed themselves with the cool, clear water.

And now I must tell you that the camels have had nothing to drink since they left the old home. The camel has a deep bag below his throat, which he fills with water enough to last four or five days; so he can travel in the desert as long as that, and sometimes longer, without drinking again. Yet I believe the camels are as glad as the children to come to the fresh spring.

Gemila thinks so at night, as she stands under the starlight, patting her good camel Simel, and kissing his great lips.

The black goats, with long silky ears, are already cropping the grass. The father sits again at the tent-door, and smokes his long pipe; the children bury their bare feet in the sand, and heap it into little mounds about them; while the mother is bringing out the dates and the bread and butter.

It is an easy thing for them to move: they are already at home again. But although they have so few cares, we do not wish ourselves in their place, for we love the home of our childhood, "be it ever so humble," better than roaming like an exile.

But all the time I haven't told you how Gemila looks, nor what clothes she wears. Her face is dark; she has a little straight nose, full lips, and dark, earnest eyes; her dark hair will be braided when it is long enough. On her arms and her ankles are gilded bracelets and anklets, and she wears a brown cotton dress loosely hanging halfway to the bare, slender ankles. On her head the white fringed handkerchief, of which I told you, hangs like a little veil. Her face is pleasant, and when she smiles her white teeth shine between her parted lips.

She is the child of the desert, and she loves her desert home.

I think she would hardly be happy to live in a house, eat from a table, and sleep in a little bed like yours. She would grow restless and weary if she should live so long and so quietly in one place.

The Seven Little Sisters

THE LITTLE MOUNTAIN MAIDEN.

I want you to look at the picture on this page. It is a little deer: its name is the chamois. Do you see what delicate horns it has, and what slender legs, and how it seems to stand on that bit of rock and lift its head to watch for the hunters.

Last summer I saw a little chamois like that, and just as small: it was not alive, but cut or carved of wood,—such a graceful pretty little plaything as one does not meet every day.

Would you like to know who made it, and where it came from?

It was made in the mountain country, by the brother of my good
Jeannette, the little Swiss maiden.

Here among the high mountains she lives with her father, mother, and brothers; and far up among those high snowy peaks, which are seen behind the house, the chamois live, many of them together, eating the tender grass and little pink-colored flowers, and leaping and springing away over the ice and snow when they see the men coming up to hunt them.

I will tell you by and by how it happened that Jeannette's tall brother Joseph carved this tiny chamois from wood. But first you must know about this small house upon the great hills, and how they live up there so near the blue sky.

One would think it might be easier for a child to be good and pure so far up among the quiet hills, and that there God would seem to come close to the spirit, even of a little girl or boy.

On the sides of the mountains tall trees are growing,— pine and fir trees, which are green in winter as well as in summer. If you go into the woods in winter, you will find that almost all the trees have dropped their pretty green leaves upon the ground, and are standing cold and naked in the winter wind; but the pines and the firs keep on their warm green clothes all the year round.

It was many years ago, before Jeannette was born, that her father came to the mountains with his sharp axe and cut down some of the fir-trees. Other men helped him, and they cut the great trees into strong logs and boards, and built of them the house of which I have told you. Now he will have a good home of his own for as long as he likes to live there, and to it will come his wife and children as God shall send them, to nestle among the hills.

Then he went down to the little town at the foot of the mountain, and when he came back, he was leading a brown, long-eared donkey, and upon that donkey sat a rosy-cheeked young woman, with smiling brown eyes, and long braids of brown hair hanging below a little green hat set on one side of her head, while beautiful rose-colored carnations peeped from beneath it on the other side. Who was this? It wasn't Jeannette: you know I told you this was before she was born. Can you guess, or must I tell you that it was the little girl's mother? She had come up the mountain for the first time to her new home,—the house built of the fir and the pine,—where after awhile were born Jeannette's two tall brothers, and at last Jeannette herself.

It was a good place to be born in. When she was a baby she used to lie on the short, sweet grass before the doorstep, and watch the cows and the goats feeding, and clap her little hands to see how rosy the sunset made the snow that shone on the tops of those high peaks. And the next summer, when she could run alone, she picked the blue-eyed gentians, thrusting her small fingers between their fringed eyelids, and begging them to open and look at little Jean; and she stained her wee hands among the strawberries, and pricked them with the thorns of the long raspberry-vines, when she went with her mother in the afternoon to pick the sweet fruit for supper. Ah, she was a happy little thing! Many a fall she got over the stones or among the brown moss, and many a time the clean frock that she wore was dyed red with the crushed berries; but, oh, how pleasant it was to find them in great patches on the mountain-side, where the kind sun had warmed them into such delicious life! I have seen the children run out of school to pick such sweet wild strawberries, all the recess-time, up in the fields of Maine; and how happy they were with their little stained fingers as they came back at the call of the bell!

In the black bog-mud grew the Alpen roses, and her mother said, "Do not go there, my little daughter, it is too muddy for you." But at night, when her brother came home from the chamois hunt, he took off his tall, pointed hat, and showed his little sister the long spray of roses twisted round it, which he had brought for her. He could go in the mud with his thick boots, you know, and never mind it.

Here they live alone upon the mountain; there are no near neighbors. At evening they can see the blue smoke curling from the chimney of one house that stands behind that sunny green slope, a hundred yards from their door, and they can always look down upon the many houses of the town below, where the mother lived when she was young.

Many times has Jeannette wondered how the people lived down there,—so many together; and where their cows could feed, and whether there were any little girls like herself, and if they picked berries, and had such a dear old black nanny-goat as hers, that gave milk for her supper, and now had two little black kids, its babies. She didn't know about those little children in Maine, and that they have little kids and goats, as well as sweet red berries, to make the days pass happily.

She wanted to go down and see, some day, and her father promised that, when she was a great girl, she should go down with him on market-days, to sell the goats'-milk cheeses and the sweet butter that her mother made.

When the cows and goats have eaten all the grass near the house, her father drives them before him up farther among the mountains, where more grass is growing, and there he stays with them many weeks: he does not even come home at night, but sleeps in a small hut among the rocks, where, too, he keeps the large clean milk-pails, and the little one-legged stool upon which he sits at morning and night to milk the cows and goats.

When the pails are full, the butter is to be made, and the cheese; and he works while the animals feed. The cows have little bells tied to their necks, that he may hear and find them should they stray too far.

Many times, when he is away, does his little daughter at home listen, listen, while she sits before the door, to hear the distant tinkling of the cow-bells. She is a loving little daughter, and she thinks of her father so far away alone, and wishes he was coming home to eat some of the sweet strawberries and cream for supper.

Last summer some travellers came to the house. They stopped at the door and asked for milk; the mother brought them brimming bowlsful, and the shy little girl crept up behind her mother with her birch-bark baskets of berries. The gentlemen took them and thanked her, and one told of his own little Mary at home, far away over the great sea. Jeannette often thinks of her, and wonders whether her papa has gone home to her.

While the gentlemen talked, Jeannette's brother Joseph sat upon the broad stone doorstep and listened. Presently one gentleman, turning to him, asked if he would come with them over the mountain to lead the way, for there are many wild places and high, steep rocks, and they feared to get lost.

Joseph sprang up from his low seat and said he would go, brought his tall hat and his mountain-staff, like a long, strong cane, with a sharp iron at the end, which he can stick into the snow or ice if there is danger of slipping; and they went merrily on their way, over the green grass, over the rocks, far up among the snow and ice, and the frozen streams and rivers that pour down the mountain-sides.

Joseph was brave and gay; he led the way, singing aloud until the echoes answered from every hillside. It makes one happy to sing, and when we are busy and happy we sing without thinking of it, as the birds do. When everything is bright and beautiful in nature around us, we feel like singing aloud and praising God, who made the earth so beautiful; then the earth also seems to sing of God who made it, and the echo seems like its answer of praise. Did you ever hear the echo,—the voice that seems to come from a hill or a house far away, repeating whatever you may say? Among the mountains the echoes answer each other again and again. Jeannette has often heard them.

That night, while the mother and her little girl were eating their supper, the gentlemen came back again, bringing Joseph with them. He could not walk now, nor spring from rock to rock with his Alpen staff; he had fallen and broken his leg, and he must lie still for many days. But he could keep a cheerful face, and still sing his merry songs; and as he grew better, and could sit out again on the broad bench beside the door, he took his knife and pieces of fine wood, and carved beautiful things,—first a spoon for his little sister, with gentians on the handle; then a nice bowl, with a pretty strawberry-vine carved all about the edge. And from this bowl, and with this spoon, she ate her supper every night,—sweet milk,

with the dry cakes of rye bread broken into it, and
sometimes the red strawberries. I know his little sister
loved him dearly, and thanked him in her heart every time
she used the pretty things. How dearly a sister and brother
can love each other!

Then he made other things,—knives, forks, and plates;
and at last one day he sharpened his knife very sharp,
chose a very nice, delicate piece of wood, and carved this
beautiful chamois, just like a living one, only so small.
My cousin, who was travelling there, bought it and
brought it home.

When the summer had passed, the father came down
from the high pastures; the butter and cheese making was
over, and the autumn work was now to be done. Do you
want to know what the autumn work was, and how
Jeannette could help about it? I will tell you. You must
know that a little way down the mountain-side is a grove
of chestnut-trees. Did you ever see the chestnut-trees?
They grow in our woods, and on the shores of some
ponds. In the spring they are covered with long, yellowish
blossoms, and all through the hot summer those blossoms
are at work, turning into sweet chestnuts, wrapped safely
in round, thorny balls, which will prick your fingers sadly
if you don't take care. But when the frost of the autumn
nights comes, it cracks open the prickly ball and shows a
shining brown nut inside; then, if we are careful, we may
pull off the covering and take out the nut. Sometimes,
indeed, there are two, three, or four nuts in one shell; I
have found them so myself.

Now the autumn work, which I said I would tell you
about, is to gather these chestnuts and store them away,—
some to be eaten, boiled or roasted, by the bright fire in

the cold winter days that are coming; and some to be nicely packed in great bags, and carried on the donkey down to the town to be sold. The boys of New England, too, know what good fun it is to gather nuts in the fall, and spread them over the garret floor to dry, and at last to crack and eat them by the winter hearth. So when the father says one night at supper-time, "It is growing cold; I think there will be a frost to-night," Jeannette knows very well what to do; and she dances away right early in the evening to her little bed, which is made in a wooden box built up against the side of the wall, and falls asleep to dream about the chestnut woods, and the squirrels, and the little brook that leaps and springs from rock to rock down under the tall, dark trees.

She has gone to bed early, that she may wake with the first daylight, and she is out of bed in a minute when she hears her father's cheerful call in the morning, "Come, children, it is time to be off."

Their dinner is packed in a large basket. The donkey stands ready before the door, with great empty bags hanging at each side, and they go merrily over the crisp white frost to the chestnut-trees. How the frost has opened the burrs! He has done more than half their work for them already. How they laugh and sing and shout to each other as they gather the smooth brown nuts, filling their baskets, and running to pour them into the great bags! It is merry autumn work. The sun looks down upon them through the yellow leaves, and the rocks give them mossy seats; while here and there comes a bird or a squirrel to see what these strange people are doing in their woods.

Jeannette declares that the chestnut days are the best in the year. Perhaps she is right. I am sure I should enjoy them, shouldn't you? She really helps, although she is but a little girl, and her father says at night that his little Jean is a dear, good child. It makes her very happy. She thinks of what he has said while she undresses at night, unbraiding her hair and unlacing her little blue bodice with its great white sleeves, and she goes peacefully to sleep, to dream again of the merry autumn days. And while she dreams good angels must be near her, for she said her sweet and reverent prayer on her knees, with a full and thankful heart to the All-Father who gave her so many blessings.

She is our little mountain sister. The mountain life is a fresh and happy one. I should like to stay with this little sister a long, long time.

The Seven Little Sisters

THE STORY OF PEN-SE.

Dear children, have you ever watched the sun set? If you live in the country, I am almost sure you have many times delighted yourselves with the gold and rosy clouds. But those of you who live in the city do not often have the opportunity, the high houses and narrow streets shut out so much of the sky.

I am so happy as to live in the country; and let me tell you where I go to see the sun set.

The house in which I live has some dark, narrow garret stairs leading from the third story into a small garret under the roof, and many and many a time do I go up these narrow stairs, and again up to the scuttle-window in the roof, open it, and seat myself on the top step or on the roof itself. Here I can look over the house-tops, and even over the tree-tops, seeing many things of which I may perhaps tell you at some time; but to-night we are to look at the sunset.

Can you play that you are up here with me, looking past the houses, past the elm-trees and the low hills that seem so far away, to where the sun hangs low, like a great red ball, so bright that we can hardly look at it? Watch it with me. Now a little part has disappeared; now it is half gone, and in a minute more we see nothing but the train of bright clouds it has left behind.

Where did it go?

It seemed to slip down over the edge of the world. To-morrow morning, if you are up early, you will see it come back again on the other side. As it goes away from us to-night, it is coming to somebody who lives far away, round the other side of the world. While we had the sunshine, she had night; and now, when night is coming to us, it is morning for her.

I think men have always felt like following the sun to the unknown West, beyond its golden gate of setting day, and perhaps that has led many a wanderer on his path of discovery. Let us follow the sun over the rolling earth.

The sun has gone; shall we go, too, and take a peep round there to see who is having morning now?

The long, bright sunbeams are sliding over the tossing ocean, and sparkling on the blue water of a river upon which are hundreds of boats. The boats are not like those which we see here, with white sails or long oars. They are clumsy, square-looking things, without sails, and they have little sheds or houses built upon them. We will look into one, and see what is to be seen.

There is something like a little yard built all around this boat; in it are ducks,—more ducks than you can well count. This is their bedroom, where they sleep at night;

but now it is morning, and they are all stirring,—waddling about as well as they can in the crowd, and quacking with most noisy voices. They are waking up Kang-hy, their master, who lives in the middle of the boat; and out he comes from the door of his odd house, and out comes little Pen-se, his daughter, who likes to see the ducks go for their breakfast.

The father opens a gate or door in the basket-work fence of the ducks' house, and they all crowd and hurry to reach the water again, after staying all night shut up in this cage. There they go, tumbling and diving. Each must have a thorough bath first of all; then the old drake leads the way, and they swim off in the bright water along the shore for a hundred yards, and then among the marshes, where they will feed all day, and come back at night when they hear the shrill whistle of Kang-hy calling them to come home and go to bed.

Pen-se and her father will go in to breakfast now, under the bamboo roof which slides over the middle part of the boat, or can be pushed back if they desire. As Kang-hy turns to go in, and takes off his bamboo hat, the sun shines on his bare, shaved head, where only one lock of hair is left; that is braided into a long, thick tail, and hangs far down his back. He is very proud of it, and nothing would induce him to have it cut off. Now it hangs down over his loose blue nankeen jacket, but when he goes to work he will twist it round upon the crown of his head, and tuck the end under the coil to keep it out of the way. Isn't this a funny way for a man to wear his hair? Pen-se has hers still in little soft curls, but by and by it will be braided, and at last fastened up into a high knot on the top of her head, as her mother's is. Her little brother Lin already has his head shaved almost bare, and waits impatiently for the time when his single lock of hair will be long enough to braid.

When I was a child it was a very rare thing to see people such as these in our own land, but now we are quite familiar with these odd ways of dressing, and our streets have many of these funny names on their signs.

Shall we look in to see them at breakfast? Tea for the children as well as for the father and mother. They have no milk, and do not like to drink water, so they take many cups of tea every day. And here, too, are their bowls of rice upon the table, but no spoons or forks with which to eat it. Pen-se, however, does not need spoon or fork; she takes two small, smooth sticks, and, lifting the bowl to her mouth, uses the sticks like a little shovel. You would spill the rice and soil your dress if you should try to do so, but these children know no other way, and they have learned to do it quite carefully.

The sticks are called chopsticks; and up in the great house on the hill, where Pen-se went to carry fish, lives a little lady who has beautiful pearl chopsticks, and wears roses in her hair. Pen-se often thinks of her, and wishes she might go again to carry the fish, and see some of the beautiful things in that garden with the high walls. Perhaps you have in your own house, or in your schoolroom, pictures of some of the pretty things that may have been there,—little children and ladies dressed in flowery gowns, with fans in their hands; tea-tables and pretty dishes, and a great many lovely flowers and beautiful birds.

But now she must not stop to think. Breakfast is over, and the father must go on shore to his work,—carrying

tea-boxes to the store of a great merchant. Lin, too, goes
to his work, of which I will by and by tell you; and even
Pen-se and her little sister, young as they are, must go
with their mother, who has a tanka-boat in which she
carries fresh fruit and vegetables, to the big ships which
are lying off shore. The two little girls can help at the
oars, while the mother steers to guide the boat.

I wish I could tell you how pleasant it is out on the
river this bright morning. A hundred boats are moving;
the ducks and geese have all gone up the stream; the
people who live in the boats have breakfasted, and the
fishermen have come out to their work. This is Lin's
work. He works with his uncle Chow, and already his
blue trousers are stripped above his knees, and he stands
on the wet fishing-raft watching some brown birds.
Suddenly one of them plunges into the water and brings
up a fish in its yellow bill. Lin takes it out and sends the
bird for another; and such industrious fishermen are the
brown cormorants that they keep Lin and his uncle busy
all the morning, until the two large baskets are filled with
fish, and then the cormorants may catch for themselves.
Lin brings his bamboo pole, rests it across his shoulders,
hangs one basket on each end, and goes up into the town
to sell his fish. Here it was that Pen-se went on that happy
day when she saw the little lady in the house on the hill,
and she has not forgotten the wonders of that day in the
streets.

The gay sign-posts in front of the shops, with colors
flying; the busy workmen,—tinkers mending or making
their wares; blacksmiths with all their tools set up at the
corners of the streets; barbers with grave faces, intently
braiding the long hair of their customers; water-carriers
with deep water-buckets hung from a bamboo pole like

Lin's fish-baskets; the soldiers in their paper helmets, wadded gowns, and quilted petticoats, with long, clumsy guns over their shoulders; and learned scholars in brown gowns, blue bordered, and golden birds on their caps. The high officers, cousins to the emperor, have the sacred yellow girdle round their waists, and very long braided tails hanging below their small caps. Here and there you may see a high, narrow box, resting on poles, carried by two men. It is the only kind of carriage which you will see in these streets, and in it is a lady going out to take the air; although I am sadly afraid she gets but little, shut up there in her box. I would rather be like Pen-se, a poor, hardworking little girl, with a fresh life on the river, and a hard mat spread for her bed in the boat at night. How would you like to live in a boat on a pleasant river with the ducks and geese? I think you would have a very jolly time, rocked to sleep by the tide, and watched over by the dancing boat-lights. But this poor lady couldn't walk, or enjoy much, if she were allowed. Shall I tell you why? When she was a very little girl, smaller than you are, smaller than Pen-se is now, her soft baby feet were bound up tightly, the toes turned and pressed under, and the poor little foot cramped so that she could scarcely stand. This was done that her feet might never grow large, for in this country on the other side of the world one is considered very beautiful who has small feet; and now that she is a grown lady, as old perhaps as your mamma, she wears such little shoes you would think them too small for yourself. It is true they are very pretty shoes, made of bright-colored satin, and worked all over with gold and silver thread, and they have beautiful white soles of rice-paper; and the poor lady looks down at them and says to herself proudly, "Only three inches long." And forgetting how much the bandages pained her, and not thinking how sad it is only to be able to hobble about a little, instead of running and leaping as children should, she binds up the feet of Lou, her dear little daughter, in the great house on the hill, and makes her a poor, helpless child; not so happy, with all her flower-gardens, gold and silver fish, and beautiful gold-feathered birds, as Pen-se with her broad, bare feet, and comfortable, fat little toes, as she stands in the wet tanka-boat, helping her mother wash it with river-water, while the leather shoes of both of them lie high and dry on the edge of the wharf, until the wet work is done.

But we are forgetting Lin, who has carried his fish up into the town to sell. Here is a whole street where nothing is sold but food. I should call it Market Street, and I dare say they do the same in a way of their own.

What will all these busy people have for dinner to-day? Fat bears'-paws, brought from the dark forest fifty miles away,—these will do for that comfortable-looking mandarin with the red ball on the top of his cap. I think he has eaten something of the same kind before. A birds'-nest soup for my lady in the great house on the hill; birds' nests brought from the rocks where the waves dash, and the birds feel themselves very safe. But "Such a delicious soup!" said Madam Faw-Choo, and Yang-lo, her son, sent the fisherman again to the black rocks for more.

What will the soldiers have,—the officer who wears thick satin boots, and doesn't look much like fighting in his gay silk dress? A stew of fat puppies for him, and only boiled rats for the porter who carries the heavy tea-boxes. But there is tea for all, and rice, too, as much as they desire; and, although I shouldn't care to be invited to dine with any of them, I don't doubt they enjoy the food very much.

The Seven Little Sisters

In the midst of all this buying and selling Lin sells his fish, some to the English gentleman, and some to the grave-faced man in the blue gown; and he goes happily home to his own dinner in the boat. Rice again, and fried mice, and the merry face and small, slanting black eyes of his little sister to greet him. After dinner his father has a pipe to smoke, before he goes again to his work. After all, why not eat puppies and mice as well as calves and turtles and oysters? And as for birds'-nest soup, I should think it quite as good as chicken pie. It is only custom that makes any difference.

So pass the days of our child Pen-se, who lives on the great river which men call the child of the ocean. But it was not always so. She was born among the hills where the tea grows with its glossy, myrtle-like leaves, and white, fragrant blossoms. When the tea-plants were in bloom, Pen-se first saw the light; and when she was hardly more than a baby she trotted behind her father, while he gathered the leaves, dried and rolled them, and then packed them in square boxes to come in ships across the ocean for your papa and mine to drink.

Here, too, grew the mulberry-trees, with their purple fruit and white; and Pen-se learned to know and to love the little worms that eat the mulberry-leaves, and then spin for themselves a silken shell, and fall into a long sleep inside of it. She watched her mother spin off the fine silk and make it into neat skeins, and once she rode on her mother's back to market to sell it. You could gather mulberry-leaves, and set up these little silkworm boxes on the windowsill of your schoolroom. I have seen silk and flax and cotton all growing in a pleasant schoolroom, to show the scholars of what linen and silk and cotton are made.

~ 56 ~

Now those days are all past. She can hardly remember them, she was so little then; and she has learned to be happy in her new home on the river, where they came when the fire burned their house, and the tea-plants and the mulberry-trees were taken by other men.

Sometimes at night, after the day's work is over, the ducks have come home, and the stars have come out, she sits at the door of the boat-house, and watches the great bright fireflies over the marshes, and thinks of the blue lake Syhoo, covered with lilies, where gilded boats are sailing, and the people seem so happy.

Up in the high-walled garden of the great house on the hill, the night-moths have spread their broad, soft wings, and are flitting among the flowers, and the little girl with the small feet lies on her silken bed, half asleep. She, too, thinks of the lake and the lilies, but she knows nothing about Pen-se, who lives down upon the river.

See, the sun has gone from them. It must be morning for us now.

The Seven Little Sisters

Jane Andrew

THE LITTLE DARK GIRL.

In this part of the world, Manenko would certainly be considered a very wild little girl. I wonder how you would enjoy her for a playmate. She has never been to school, although she is more than seven years old, and doesn't know how to read, or even to tell her letters; she has never seen a book but once, and she has never learned to sew or to knit.

If you should try to play at paper dolls with her, she would make very funny work with the dresses, I assure you. Since she never wore a gown or bonnet or shoes herself, how should she know how to put them on to the doll? But, if she had a doll like herself, I am sure she would be as fond of it as you are of yours; and it would be a very cunning little dolly, I should think. Perhaps you have one that looks somewhat like this little girl in the picture.

Now I will tell you of some things which she can do.

She can paddle the small canoe on the river; she can help to hoe the young corn, and can find the wild bees' honey in the woods, gather the scarlet fruit when it is fully ripe and falls from the trees, and help her mother to pound the corn in the great wooden mortar. All this, and much more, as you will see, Manenko can do; for every little girl on the round world can help her mother, and do many useful things.

Would you like to know more of her,—how she looks, and where she lives, and what she does all day and all night?

Here is a little round house, with low doorways, most like those of a dog's house; you see we should have to stoop in going in. Look at the round, pointed roof, made of the long rushes that grow by the river, and braided together firmly with strips of mimosa-bark; fine, soft grass is spread all over this roof to keep out the rain.

If you look on the roof of the house across the street you will see that it is covered with strips of wood called shingles, which are laid one over the edge of the other; and when it is a rainy day you can see how the rain slips and slides off from these shingles, and runs and drips away from the spout.

Now, on this little house where Manenko lives there are no shingles, but the smooth, slippery grass is almost as good; and the rain slides over it and drips away, hardly ever coming in to wet the people inside, or the hard beds made of rushes, like the roof, and spread upon the floor of earth.

In this house lives Manenko, with Maunka her mother, Sekomi her father, and Zungo and Shobo her two brothers.

They are all very dark, darker than the brown baby. I believe you would call them black, but they are not really quite so. Their lips are thick, their noses broad, and instead of hair, their heads are covered with wool, such as you might see on a black sheep. This wool is braided and twisted into little knots and strings all over their heads, and bound with bits of red string, or any gay-looking thread. They think it looks beautiful, but I am afraid we should not agree with them.

Now we will see what clothes they wear.

You remember Agoonack, who wore the white bear's-skin, because she lived in the very cold country; and the little brown baby, who wore nothing but a string of beads, because she lived in the warm country. Manenko, too, lives in a warm country, and wears no clothes; but on her arms and ankles are bracelets and anklets, with little bits of copper and iron hanging to them, which tinkle as she walks; and she also, like the brown baby, has beads for her neck.

Her father and mother, and Zungo her brother, have aprons and mantles of antelope skins; and they, too, wear bracelets and anklets like hers.

Little Shobo is quite a baby and runs in the sunshine, like his little sister, without clothes. Dear little Shobo! how funny and happy he must look, and how fond he must be of his little sister, and our little sister, Manenko! We have all seen such little dark brothers and sisters. His short, soft wool is not yet braided or twisted, but crisps in little close curls all over his head.

The Seven Little Sisters

In the morning they must be up early, for the father is going to hunt, and Zungo will go with him. The mother prepares the breakfast, small cakes of bread made from the pounded corn, scarlet beans, eaten with honey, and plenty of milk from the brown cow. She brings it in a deep jug, and they dip in their hands for spoons.

All the meat is eaten, and to-day the men must go out over the broad, grassy fields for more. They will find the beautiful young antelope, so timid and gentle as to be far more afraid of you than you would be of them. They are somewhat like small deer, striped and spotted, and they have large, dark eyes, so soft and earnest you cannot help loving them. Here, too, are the buffalo, like large cows and oxen with strong horns, and the great elephants with long trunks and tusks. Sometimes even a lion is to be met, roused from his sleep by the noise of the hunters; for the lion sleeps in the daytime and generally walks abroad only at night. When you are older you can read the stories of famous lion and elephant hunters, and of strange and thrilling adventures in the "Dark Continent."

It would be a wonderful thing to you and me to see all these strange or beautiful animals, but Zungo and his father have seen them so many times that they are thinking only of the meat they will bring home, and, taking their long spears and the basket of ground nuts and meal which the mother has made ready, they are off with other hunters before the sun is up.

Now the mother takes her hoe, and, calling her little girl to help, hoes the young corn which is growing on the round hill behind the house. I must tell you something about the little hill. It looks like any other hill, you would think, and could hardly believe that there is anything very wonderful to tell about it. But listen to me.

A great many years ago there was no hill there at all, and the ground was covered with small white ants. You have seen the little ant-houses many a time on the garden-path, and all the ants at work, carrying grains of sand in their mouths, and running this way and that, as if they were busy in the most important work. Oh, the little ants are very wise! They seem to know how to contrive great things and are never idle. "Go to the ant; consider her ways, and be wise," said one of the world's wisest men.

Well, on the spot where this hill now stands the white ants began to work. They were not satisfied with small houses like those which we have seen, but they worked day after day, week after week, and even years, until they had built this hill higher than the house in which I live, and inside it is full of chambers and halls, and wonderful arched passages. They built this great house, but they do not live there now. I don't know why they moved,— perhaps because they didn't like the idea of having such near neighbors when Sekomi began to build his hut before their door. But, however it was, they went, and, patient little creatures that they are, built another just like it a mile or so away; and Sekomi said: "The hill is a fine place to plant my early corn."

There is but little hoeing to do this morning, and, while the work goes on, Shobo, the baby, rolls in the grass, sucking a piece of sugar-cane, as I have seen children suck a stick of candy. Haven't you?

The mother has baskets to make. On the floor of the hut is a heap of fine, twisting tree-roots which she brought from the forest yesterday, and under the shadow of her grassy roof she sits before the door weaving them into strong, neat baskets, like the one in which the men carried

their dinner when they went to hunt. While she works
other women come too with their work, sit beside her in
the shade, and chatter away in a very queer-sounding
language. We couldn't understand it at all; but we should
hear them always call Manenko's mother Ma-Zungo,
meaning Zungo's mother, instead of saying Maunka,
which you remember I told you is her name. Zungo is her
oldest boy, you know, and ever since he was born she has
been called nothing but Ma-Zungo,—just as if, when a
lady comes into your school, the teacher should say: "This
is Joe's mother," or "This is Teddy's mamma," so that the
children should all know her.

So the mother works on the baskets and talks with the
women; but Manenko has heard the call of the honey-
bird, the brisk little chirp of "Chiken, chiken, chik, churr,
churr," and she is away to the wood to follow his call, and
bring home the honey.

She runs beneath the tall trees, looking up for the small
brown bird; then she stops and listens to hear him again,
when close beside her comes the call, "Chiken, chiken,
chik, churr, churr," and there sits the brown bird above a
hole in the tree, where the bees are flying in and out, their
legs yellow with honey-dust. It is too high for Manenko to
reach, but she marks the place and says to herself: "I will
tell Ra when he comes home." Who is Ra? Why, that is
her name for "father." She turns to go home, but stops to
listen to the wild shouts and songs of the women who
have left the huts and are coming down towards the river
to welcome their chief with lulliloo, praising him by such
strange names as "Great lion," "Great buffalo."

The chief comes from a long journey with the young
men up the river in canoes, to hunt the elephant, and bring
home the ivory tusks, from which we have many beautiful

things made. The canoes are full of tusks, and, while the men unload them, the women are shouting: "Sleep, my lord, my great chief." Manenko listens while she stands under the trees,—listens for only a minute, and then runs to join her mother and add her little voice to the general noise.

The chief is very proud and happy to bring home such a load; before sunset it will all be carried up to the huts, the men will dress in their very best, and walk in a gay procession. Indeed, they can't dress much; no coats or hats or nicely polished boots have they to put on, but some will have the white ends of oxen's tails in their hair, some a plume of black ostrich feathers, and the chief himself has a very grand cap made from the yellow mane of an old lion. The drum will beat, the women will shout, while the men gather round a fire, and roast and eat great slices of ox-meat, and tell the story of their famous elephant-hunt. How they came to the bushes with fine, silvery leaves and sweet bark, which the elephant eats, and there hiding, watched and waited many hours, until the ground shook, with the heavy tread of a great mother-elephant and her two calves, coming up from the river, where they had been to drink. Their trunks were full of water, and they tossed them up, spouting the water like a fine shower-bath over their hot heads and backs, and now, cooled and refreshed, began to eat the silvery leaves of the bushes. Then the hunters threw their spears thick and fast; after two hours, the great creature lay still upon the ground,—she was dead.

So day after day they had hunted, loading the canoes with ivory, and sailing far up the river; far up where the tall rushes wave, twisted together by the twining morning-glory vines; far up where the alligators make great nests in the river-bank, and lay their eggs, and stretch themselves in the sunshine, half asleep inside their scaly armor; far up where the hippopotamus is standing in his drowsy dream on the bottom of the river, with the water covering him, head and all. He is a great, sleepy fellow, not unlike a very large, dark-brown pig, with a thick skin and no hair. Here he lives under the water all day, only once in a while poking up his nose for a breath of fresh air. And here is the mother-hippopotamus, with her baby standing upon her neck, that he may be nearer the top of the water. Think how funny he must look.

All day long they stand here under the water, half asleep, sometimes giving a loud grunt or snore, and sometimes, I am sorry to say, tipping over a canoe which happens to float over their heads. But at night, when men are asleep, the great beasts come up out of the river and eat the short, sweet grass upon the shore, and look about to see the world a little. Oh, what mighty beasts! Men are so small and weak beside them. And yet, because the mind of man is so much above theirs, he can rule them; for God made man to be king of the whole earth, and greater than all.

All these wonderful things the men have seen, and Manenko listens to their stories until the moon is high and the stars have almost faded in her light. Then her father and Zungo come home, bringing the antelope and buffalo meat, too tired to tell their story until the next day. So, after eating supper, they are all soon asleep upon the mats which form their beds. It is a hard kind of bed, but a good one, if you don't have too many mice for bedfellows. A little bright-eyed mouse is a pretty creature, but one doesn't care to sleep with him.

These are simple, happy people; they live out of doors most of the time, and they love the sunshine, the rain, and the wind. They have plenty to eat,—the pounded corn, milk and honey, and scarlet beans, and the hunters bring meat, and soon it will be time for the wild water-birds to come flocking down the river,—white pelicans and brown ducks, and hundreds of smaller birds that chase the skimming flies over the water.

If Manenko could read, she would be sorry that she has no books; and if she knew what dolls are, she might be longing every day for a beautiful wax doll, with curling hair, and eyes to open and shut. But these are things of which she knows nothing at all, and she is happy enough in watching the hornets building their hanging nests on the branches of the trees, cutting the small sticks of sugar-cane, or following the honey-bird's call.

If the children who have books would oftener leave them, and study the wonders of the things about them,—of the birds, the plants, the curious creatures that live and work on the land and in the air and water,—it would be better for them. Try it, dear children; open your eyes and look into the ways and forms of life in the midst of which God has placed you, and get acquainted with them, till you feel that they, too, are your brothers and sisters, and God your Father and theirs.

The Seven Little Sisters

Jane Andrew

LOUISE, THE CHILD OF THE BEAUTIFUL RIVER RHINE.

Have you heard of the beautiful River Rhine—how at first it hides, a little brook among the mountains and dark forests, and then steals out into the sunshine, and leaps down the mountain-side, and hurries away to the sea, growing larger and stronger as it runs, curling and eddying among the rocks, and sweeping between the high hills where the grape-vines grow and the solemn old castles stand?

How people come from far and near to see and to sail upon the beautiful river! And the children who are so blessed as to be born near it, and to play on its shores through all the happy young years of their lives, although they may go far away from it in the after years, never, never forget the dear and beautiful River Rhine.

It is only a few miles away from the Rhine—perhaps too far for you to walk, but not too far for me—that we shall find a fine large house, a house with pleasant gardens about it, broad gravel walks, and soft, green grass-plats to play upon, and gay flowering trees and bushes, while the rose-vines are climbing over the piazza, and opening rose-buds are peeping in at the chamber windows.

Isn't this a pleasant house? I wish we could all live in as charming a home, by as blue and lovely a river, and with as large and sweet a garden, or, if we might have such a place for our school, how delightful it would be!

Here lives Louise, my blue-eyed, sunny-haired little friend, and here in the garden she plays with Fritz and sturdy little Gretchen. And here, too, at evening the father and mother come to sit on the piazza among the roses, and the children leave their games, to nestle together on the steps while the dear brother Christian plays softly and sweetly on his flute.

Louise is a motherly child, already eight years old, and always willing and glad to take care of the younger ones; indeed, she calls Gretchen *her* baby, and the little one loves dearly her child-mamma.

They live in this great house, and they have plenty of toys and books, and plenty of good food, and comfortable little beds to sleep in at night, although, like Jeannette's, they are only neat little boxes built against the side of the wall.

But near them, in the valley, live the poor people, in small, low houses. They eat black bread, wear coarse clothes, and even the children must work all day that they may have food for to-morrow.

The mother of Louise is a gentle, loving woman; she says to her children: "Dear children, to-day we are rich, we can have all that we want, but we will not forget the poor. You may some day be poor yourselves, and, if you learn now what poverty is, you will be more ready to meet it when it comes." So, day after day, the great stove in the kitchen is covered with stew-pans and kettles, in which are cooking dinners for the sick and the poor, and day after day, as the dinner-hour draws near, Louise will come, and Fritz, and even little Gretchen, saying: "Mother, may I go?" "May I go?" and the mother answers: "Dear children, you shall all go together"; and she fills the bowls and baskets, and sends her sunny-hearted children down into the valley to old Hans the gardener, who has been lame with rheumatism so many years; and to young Marie, the pale, thin girl, who was so merry and rosy-cheeked in the vineyard a year ago; and to the old, old woman with the brown, wrinkled face and bowed head, who sits always in the sunshine before the door, and tries to knit; but the needles drop from the poor trembling hands, and the stitches slip off, and she cannot see to pick them up. She is too deaf to hear the children as they come down the road, and she is nodding her poor old head, and feeling about in her lap for the lost needle, when Louise, with her bright eyes, spies it, picks it up, and before the old woman knows she has come, a soft little hand is laid in the brown, wrinkled one, and the little girl is shouting in her ear that she has brought some dinner from mamma. It makes a smile shine in the old half-blind eyes. It is always the happiest part of the day to her when the dear little lady comes with her dinner. And it made Louise happy too, for nothing repays us so well as what we do unselfishly for others.

These summer days are full of delight for the children. It is not all play for them, to be sure; but then, work is often even more charming than play, as I think some little girls know when they have been helping their mothers,—running of errands, dusting the furniture, and sewing little squares of patchwork that the baby may have a cradle-quilt made entirely by her little sister.

Louise can knit, and, indeed, every child and woman in that country knits. You would almost laugh to see how gravely the little girl takes out her stocking, for she has really begun her first stocking, and sits on the piazza-steps for an hour every morning at work. Then the little garden, which she calls her own, must be weeded. The gardener would gladly do it, but Louise has a hoe of her own, which her father bought in the spring, and, bringing it to his little daughter, said: "Let me see how well my little girl can take care of her own garden." And the child has tried very hard; sometimes, it is true, she would let the weeds grow pretty high before they were pulled up, but, on the whole, the garden promises well, and there are buds on her moss-rose bush. It is good to take care of a garden, for, besides the pleasure the flowers can bring us, we learn how watchful we must be to root out the weeds, and how much trimming and care the plants need; so we learn how to watch over our own hearts.

She has books, too, and studies a little each day,—studies at home with her mother, for there is no school near enough for her to go to it, and while she and Fritz are so young, their mother teaches them, while Christian, who is already more than twelve years old, has gone to the school upon that beautiful hill which can be seen from Louise's chamber window,—the school where a hundred boys and girls are studying music. For, ever since he was a baby, Christian has loved music; he has sung the very sweetest little songs to Louise, while she was yet so young as to lie in her cradle, and he has whistled until the birds among the bushes would answer him again, and now, when he comes home from school to spend some long summer Sunday, he always brings the flute, and plays, as I told you in the beginning of the story.

When the summer days are over, what comes next? You do not surely forget the autumn, when the leaves of the maples turn crimson and yellow, and the oaks are red and brown, and you scuff your feet along the path ankle-deep in fallen leaves!

On the banks of the Rhine the autumn is not quite like ours. You shall see how our children of the great house will spend an autumn day.

Their father and mother have promised to go with them to the vineyards as soon as the grapes are ripe enough for gathering, and on this sunny September morning the time has really come.

In the great covered baskets are slices of bread and German sausage, bottles of milk and of beer, and plenty of fresh and delicious prunes, for the prune orchards are loaded with ripe fruit. This is their dinner, for they will not be home until night.

Oh, what a charming day for the children! Little Gretchen is rolling in the grass with delight, while Louise runs to bring her own little basket, in which to gather grapes.

They must ride in the broad old family carriage, for the little ones cannot walk so far; but, when they reach the river, they will take a boat with white sails, and go down to where the steep steps and path lead up on the other side, up the sunny green bank to the vineyard, where already the peasant girls have been at work ever since sunrise. Here the grapes are hanging in heavy, purple clusters; the sun has warmed them through and through, and made them sweet to the very heart. Oh, how delicious they are, and how beautiful they look, heaped up in the tall baskets, which the girls and women are carrying on their heads! How the children watch these peasant-girls, all dressed in neat little jackets, and many short skirts one above another, red and blue, white and green. On their heads are the baskets of grapes, and they never drop nor spill them, but carry them steadily down the steep, narrow path to the great vats, where the young men stand on short ladders to reach the top, and pour in the purple fruit. Then the grapes are crushed till the purple juice runs out, and that is wine,—such wine as even the children may drink in their little silver cups, for it is even better than milk. You may be sure that they have some at dinner-time, when they cluster round the flat rock below the dark stone castle, with the warm noonday sun streaming across their mossy table, and the mother opens the basket and gives to every one a share.

Below them is the river, with its boats and beautiful shining water; behind them are the vine-covered walls of that old castle where two hundred years ago lived armed knights and stately ladies; and all about them is the rich September air, full of the sweet fragrance of the grapes, and echoing with the songs and laughter of the grape-gatherers. On their rocky table are purple bunches of fruit, in their cups the new wine-juice, and in their hearts all the joy of the merry grape season.

There are many days like this in the autumn, but the frost will come at last, and the snow too. This is winter, but winter brings the best pleasure of all.

When two weeks of the winter had nearly passed, the children, as you may suppose, began to think of Christmas, and, indeed, their best and most loving friend had been preparing for them the sweetest of Christmas presents. Ten days before Christmas it came, however. Can you guess what it was? Something for all of them,— something which Christian will like just as well as little Gretchen will, and the father and mother will perhaps be more pleased than any one else.

Do you know what it is? What do you think of a little baby brother,—a little round, sweet, blue-eyed baby brother as a Christmas present for them all?

When Christmas Eve came, the mother said: "The children must have their Christmas-tree in my room, for baby is one of the presents, and I don't think I can let him be carried out and put upon the table in the hall, where we had it last year."

So all day long the children are kept away from their mother's room. Their father comes home with his great coat-pockets very full of something, but, of course, the children don't know what. He comes and goes, up stairs and down, and, while they are all at play in the snow, a fine young fir-tree is brought in and carried up. Louise knows it, for she picked up a fallen branch upon the stairs, but she doesn't tell Fritz and Gretchen.

How they all wait and long for the night to come! They sit at the windows, watching the red sunset light upon the snow, and cannot think of playing or eating their supper. The parlor door is open, and all are waiting and listening. A little bell rings, and in an instant there is a scampering up the broad stairs to the door of mother's room; again the

little bell rings, and the door is opened wide by their
father, who stands hidden behind it.

At the foot of their mother's white-curtained bed stands
the little fir-tree; tiny candles are burning all over it like
little stars, and glittering golden fruits are hanging among
the dark-green branches. On the white-covered table are
laid Fritz's sword and Gretchen's big doll, they being too
heavy for the tree to hold. Under the branches Louise
finds charming things; such a little work-box as it is a
delight to see, with a lock and key, and inside, thimble
and scissors, and neat little spools of silk and thread. Then
there are the fairy stories of the old Black Forest, and that
most charming of all little books, "The White Cat," and an
ivory cup and ball for Fritz. Do you remember where the
ivory comes from? And, lest Baby Hans should think
himself forgotten, there is an ivory rattle for him.

There he lies in the nurse's arms, his blue eyes wide
open with wonder, and in a minute the children, with arms
full of presents, have gathered round the old woman's
arm-chair,—gathered round the best and sweetest little
Christmas present of all. And the happy mother, who sits
up among the pillows, taking her supper, while she
watches her children, forgets to eat, and leaves the gruel
to grow cold, but her heart is warm enough.

Why is not Christian here to-night? In the school of
music, away on the hill, he is singing a grand Christmas
hymn, with a hundred young voices to join him. It is very
grand and sweet, full of thanks and of love. It makes the
little boy feel nearer to all his loved ones, and in his heart
he is thanking the dear Father who has given them that
best little Christmas present,—the baby.

Jane Andrew

LOUISE, THE CHILD OF THE WESTERN FOREST.

There are many things happening in this world, dear children,—things that happen to you yourselves day after day, which you are too young to understand at the time. By and by, when you grow to be as old as I am, you will remember and wonder about them all.

Now, it was just one of these wonderful things, too great for the young children to understand, that happened to our little Louise and her brothers and sister when the Christmas time had come around again, and the baby was more than a year old.

It was a cold, stormy night; there were great drifts of snow, and the wind was driving it against the windows. In the beautiful great parlor, beside the bright fire, sat the sweet, gentle mother, and in her lap lay the stout little Hans. The children had their little chairs before the fire, and watched the red and yellow flames, while Louise had already taken out her knitting-work.

They were all very still, for their father seemed sad and troubled, and the children were wondering what could be the matter. Their mother looked at them and smiled, but, after all, it was only a sad smile. I think it is hardest for the father, when he can no longer give to wife and children their pleasant home; but, if they can be courageous and happy when they have to give it up, it makes his heart easier and brighter.

"I must tell the children' to-night," said the father, looking at his wife, and she answered quite cheerfully: "Yes, tell them; they will not be sad about it I know."

So the father told to his wondering little ones that he had lost all his money; the beautiful great house and gardens were no longer his, and they must all leave their pleasant home near the Rhine, and cross the great, tossing ocean, to find a new home among the forests or the prairies.

As you may suppose, the children didn't fully understand this. I don't think you would yourself. You would be quite delighted with the packing and moving, and the pleasant journey in the cars, and the new and strange things you would see on board the ship, and it would be quite a long time before you could really know what it was to lose your own dear home.

So the children were not sad; you know their mother said they would not be. But when they were safely tucked up in their little beds, and tenderly kissed by the most loving lips, Louise could not go to sleep for thinking of this strange moving, and wondering what they should carry, and how long they should stay. For she had herself once been on a visit to her uncle in the city, carrying her clothes in a new little square trunk, and riding fifty miles in the cars, and she thought it would be quite a fine thing that they should all pack up trunks full of clothing, and go together on even a longer journey.

A letter had been written to tell Christian, and the next day he came home from the school. His uncles in the city begged him to stay with them, but the boy said earnestly: "If my father must cross the sea, I too must go with him."

They waited only for the winter's cold to pass away, and when the first robins began to sing among the naked trees, they had left the fine large house,—left the beautiful gardens where the children used to play, left the great, comfortable arm-chairs and sofas, the bookcases and tables, and the little beds beside the wall. Besides their clothes, they had taken nothing with them but two great wooden chests full of beautiful linen sheets and table-cloths. These had been given to the mother by her mother long ago, before any of the children were born, and they must be carried to the new home. You will see, by and by, how glad the family all were to have them.

Did you ever go on board a ship? It is almost like a great house upon the water, but the rooms in it are very small, and so are the windows. Then there is the long deck, where we may walk in the fresh air and watch the water and the sea-birds, or the sailors at work upon the high masts among the ropes, and the white sails that spread out like a white bird's wings, and sweep the ship along over the water.

It was in such a ship that our children found themselves, with their father and mother, when the snow was gone and young grass was beginning to spring up on the land. But of this they could see nothing, for in a day they had flown on the white wings far out over the water, and as Louise clung to her father's hand and stood upon the deck at sunset, she saw only water and sky all about on every side, and the red clouds of the sunset. It was a little sad, and quite strange to her, but her younger brothers and sisters were already asleep in the small beds of the ship, which, as perhaps you know, are built up against the wall, just as their beds were at home. Louise kissed her father and went down, too, to bed, for you must know that on board ship you go *down* stairs to bed instead of *up* stairs.

After all, if father, mother, brother, and sister can still cling to each other and love each other, it makes little difference where they are, for love is the best thing in the universe, and nothing is good without it.

They lived for many days in the ship, and the children, after a little time, were not afraid to run about the deck and talk with the sailors, who were always very kind to them. And Louise felt quite at home sitting in her little chair beside the great mast, while she knit upon her stocking,—a little stocking now, one for the baby.

Christian had brought his flute, and at night he played to them as he used at home, and, indeed, they were all so loving and happy together that it was not much sorrow to lose the home while they kept each other.

Sometimes a hard day would come, when the clouds swept over them, and the rain and the great waves tossed the ship, making them all sick, and sad too, for a time; but the sun was sure to come out at last, as I can assure you it always will, and, on the whole, it was a pleasant journey for them all.

It was a fine, sunny May day when they reached the land again. No time, though, for them to go Maying, for only see how much is to be done! Here are all the trunks and the linen-chests, and all the children, too, to be disposed of, and they are to stop but two days in this city. Then they must be ready for a long journey in the cars and steamboats, up rivers and across lakes, and sometimes for miles and miles through woods, where they see no houses nor people, excepting here and there a single log cabin with two or three ragged children at play outside, or a baby creeping over the doorstep, while farther on among the trees stands a man with his axe, cutting, with heavy blows, some tall trees into such logs as those of which the house is built.

These are new and strange sights to the children of the River Rhine. They wonder, and often ask their parents if they, too, shall live in a little log house like that.

How fresh and fragrant the new logs are for the dwelling, and how sweet the pine and spruce boughs for a bed! A good new log house in the green woods is the best home in the world.

Oh, how heartily tired they all are when at last they stop! They have been riding by day and by night. The children have fallen asleep with heads curled down upon their arms upon the seats of the car, and the mother has had very hard work to keep little Hans contented and happy. But here at last they have stopped. Here is the new home.

They have left the cars at a very small town. It has ten or twelve houses and one store, and they have taken here a great wagon with three horses to carry them yet a few miles farther to a lonely, though beautiful place. It is on the edge of a forest. The trees are very tall, their trunks moss-covered; and when you look far in among them it is so dark that no sunlight seems to fall on the brown earth. But outside is sunshine, and the young spring grass and wild flowers, different from those which grow on the Rhine banks.

But where is their house?

Here is indeed something new for them. It is almost night; no house is near, and they have no sleeping-place but the great wagon. But their cheerful mother packs them all away in the back part of the wagon, on some straw, covering them with shawls as well as she can, and bids them good-night, saying, "You can see the stars whenever you open your eyes."

It is a new bed and a hard one. However, the children are tired enough to sleep well; but they woke very early, as you or I certainly should if we slept in the great concert-hall of the birds. Oh, how those birds of the woods did begin to sing, long before sunrise! And Christian was out from his part of the bed in a minute, and off four miles to the store, to buy some bread for breakfast.

An hour after sunrise he was back again, and Louise had gathered sticks, of which her father made a bright fire. And now the mother is teaching her little daughter how to make tea, and Fritz and Gretchen are poking long sticks into the ashes to find the potatoes which were hidden there to roast.

To them it is a beautiful picnic, like those happy days in the grape season; but Louise can see that her mother is a little grieved at having them sleep in the wagon with no house to cover them. And when breakfast is over she says to the father that the children must be taken back to the village to stay until the house is built. He, too, had thought so; and the mother and children go back to the little town.

Christian alone stays with his father, working with his small axe as his father does with the large one; but to both it is very hard work to cut trees; because it is something they have never done before. They do their best, and when he is not too tired, Christian whistles to cheer himself.

After the first day a man is hired to help, and it is not a great while before the little house is built—built of great, rough logs, still covered with brown bark and moss. All the cracks are stuffed with moss to keep out the rain and cold, and there is one window and a door.

It is a poor little house to come to after leaving the grand old one by the Rhine, but the children are delighted when their father comes with the great wagon to take them to their new home.

And into this house one summer night they come— without beds, tables, or chairs; really with nothing but the trunks and linen-chests. The dear old linen-chests, see only how very useful they have become! What shall be the supper-table for this first meal in the new house?

What but the largest of the linen-chests, round which they all gather, some sitting on blocks of wood, and the little ones standing! And after supper what shall they have for beds? What but the good old chests again! For many and many a day and night they are used, and the mother is, over and over again, thankful that she brought them.

As the summer days go by, the children pick berries in the woods and meadows, and Fritz is feeling himself a great boy when his father expects him to take care of the old horse, blind of one eye, bought to drag the loads of wood to market.

Louise is learning to love the grand old trees where the birds and squirrels live. She sits for hours with her work on some mossy cushion under the great waving boughs, and she is so silent and gentle that the squirrels learn to come very near her, turning their heads every minute to see if she is watching, and almost laughing at her with their sharp, bright eyes, while they are cramming their cheeks full of nuts—not to eat now, you know, but to carry home to the storehouses in some comfortable hollow trees, to be saved for winter use. When the snow comes, you see, they will not be able to find any nuts.

One day Louise watched them until she suddenly thought, "Why don't we, too, save nuts for the winter?" and the next day she brought a basket and the younger children, instead of her knitting-work. They frightened away the squirrels, to be sure, but they carried home a fine large basketful of nuts.

Oh, how much might be seen in those woods on a summer day!—birds and flowers, and such beautiful moss! I have seen it myself, so soft and thick, better than the softest cushion to sit on, and then so lovely to look at, with its long, bright feathers of green.

Sometimes Louise has seen the quails going out for a walk; the mother with her seven babies all tripping primly along behind her, the wee, brown birds; and all running, helter-skelter, in a minute, if they hear a noise among the bushes, and hiding, each one, his head under a broad leaf, thinking, poor little foolish things, that no one can see them.

Christian whistles to the quails a long, low call; they will look this way and that and listen, and at last really run towards him without fear.

Before winter comes the log house is made more comfortable; beds and chairs are bought, and a great fire burns in the fireplace. But do the best they can the rain will beat in between the logs, and after the first snowstorm one night, a white pointed drift is found on the breakfast-table. They laugh at it, and call it ice-cream, but they almost feel more like crying, with cold blue fingers, and toes that even the warm knit stockings can't keep comfortable. Never mind, the swift snowshoes will make them skim over the snow-crust like birds flying, and the merry sled-rides that brother Christian will give them will make up for all the trouble. They will soon love the winter in the snowy woods.

Their clothes, too, are all wearing out. Fritz comes to his mother with great holes in his jacket-sleeves, and poor Christian's knees are blue and frost-bitten through the torn trousers. What shall be done?

Louise brings out two old coats of her father's. Christian is wrapped in one from head to foot, and Fritz looks like the oddest little man with his great coat muffled around him, crossed in front and buttoned around behind, while the long sleeves can be turned back almost to his shoulders. Funny enough he looks, but it makes him quite warm; and in this biting wind who would think of the looks? So our little friend is to drive poor old Major to town with a sled-load of wood every day, while his father and brother are cutting trees in the forest.

Should you laugh to see a boy so dressed coming up the street with a load of wood? Perhaps you wouldn't if you knew how cold he would be without this coat, and how much he hopes to get the half-dollar for his wood, and bring home bread and meat for supper.

How wise the children grow in this hard work and hard life! Fritz feels himself a little man, and Louise, I am sure, is as useful as many a woman, for she is learning to cook and tend the fire, while even Gretchen has some garters to knit, and takes quite good care of the baby.

Little Hans will never remember the great house by the Rhine; he was too little when they came away; but by and by he will like to hear stories about it, which, you may be sure, Louise will often tell her little brother.

The winter is the hardest time. When Christmas comes there is not even a tree, for there are no candles to light one and no presents to give. But there is one beautiful gift which they may and do all give to each other,—it makes them happier than many toys or books,—it is love. It makes even this cold dreary Christmas bright and beautiful to them.

Next winter will not be so hard, for in the spring corn will be planted, and plenty of potatoes and turnips and cabbages; and they will have enough to eat and something to sell for money.

But I must not stay to tell you more now of the backwoods life of Louise and her brothers and sister. If you travel some day to the West, perhaps you will see her yourself, gathering her nuts under the trees, or sitting in the sun on the doorstep with her knitting. Then you will know her for the little sister who has perhaps come closest to your heart, and you will clasp each other's hands in true affection.

Jane Andrew

THE SEVEN LITTLE SISTERS.

Here, dear children, are your seven little sisters. Let us count them over. First came the brown baby, then Agoonack, Gemila, Jeannette, Pen-se, Manenko, and Louise. Seven little sisters I have called them, but Marnie exclaims: "How can they be sisters when some are black, some brown, and some white; when one lives in the warm country and another in the cold, and Louise upon the shores of the Rhine? Sallie and I are sisters, because we have the same father and live here together in the same house by the seaside; but as for those seven children, I can't believe them to be sisters at all."

Now let us suppose, my dear little girl, that your sister Sallie should go away,—far away in a ship across the ocean to the warm countries, and the sun should burn her face and hands and make them so brown that you would hardly know her,—wouldn't she still be your sister Sallie?

And suppose even that she should stay away in the warm countries and never come back again, wouldn't she still be your dear sister? and wouldn't you write her letters and tell her about home and all that you love there?

I know you would.

And now, just think if you yourself should take a great journey through ice and snow and go to the cold countries, up among the white bears and the sledges and dogs; suppose even that you should have an odd little dress of white bear-skin, like Agoonack, wouldn't you think it very strange if Sallie shouldn't call you her little sister just because you were living up there among the ice?

And what if Minnie, too, should take it into her head to sail across the seas and live in a boat on a Chinese river, like Pen-se, and drive the ducks, eat rice with chopsticks, and have fried mice for dinner; why, you might not want to dine with her, but she would be your sweet, loving sister all the same, wouldn't she?

I can hear you say "Yes" to all this, but then you will add: "Father is our father the same all the time, and he isn't Pen-se's father, nor Manenko's."

Let us see what makes you think he is your father. Because he loves you so much and gives you everything that you have—clothes to wear, and food to eat, and fire to warm you?

Did he give you this new little gingham frock? Shall we see what it is made of? If you ravel out one end of the cloth, you can find the little threads of cotton which are woven together to make your frock. Where did the cotton come from?

It grew in the hot fields of the South, where the sun shines very warmly. Your father didn't make it grow, neither did any man. It is true a man, a poor black man, and a very sad man he was too, put the little seeds into the ground, but they would never have grown if the sun hadn't shone, the soft earth nourished, and the rain moistened them. And who made the earth, and sent the sun and the rain?

That must be somebody very kind and thoughtful, to take so much care of the little cotton-seeds. I think that must be a father.

Now, what did you have for breakfast this morning?

A sweet Indian cake with your egg and mug of milk? I thought so. Who made this breakfast? Did Bridget make the cake in the kitchen? Yes, she mixed the meal with milk and salt and sugar. But where did she get the meal? The miller ground the yellow corn to make it. But who made the corn?

The seeds were planted as the cottonseeds were, and the same kind care supplied sun and rain and earth for them. Wasn't that a father? Not your father who sits at the head of the table and helps you at dinner, who takes you to walk and tells you stories, but another Father; your Father, too, he must be, for he is certainly taking care of you.

And doesn't he make the corn grow, also, on that ant-hill behind
Manenko's house? He seems to take the same care of her as of you.

Then the milk and the egg. They come from the hen and the cow; but who made the hen and the cow?

It was the same kind Father again who made them for you, and made the camels and goats for Gemila and Jeannette; who made also the wild bees, and taught them to store their honey in the trees, for Manenko; who made the white rice grow and ripen for little Pen-se, and the sea-birds and the seals for Agoonack. To every one good food to eat—and more than that; for must it not be a very loving father who has made for us all the beautiful sky, and the stars at night, and the blue sea; who sent the soft wind to rock the brown baby to sleep and sing her a song, and the grand march of the Northern Lights for Agoonack—grander and more beautiful than any of the fireworks you know; the red strawberries for little Jeannette to gather, and the beautiful chestnut woods on the mountain-side? Do you remember all these things in the stories?

And wasn't it the same tender love that made the sparkling water and sunshine for Pen-se, and the shining brown ducks for her too; the springs in the desert and the palm-trees for Gemila, as well as the warm sunshine for Manenko, and the beautiful River Rhine for Louise?

It must be a very dear father who gives his children not only all they need for food and clothing, but so many, many beautiful things to enjoy.

Don't you see that they must all be his children, and so all sisters, and that he is your Father, too, who makes the mayflowers bloom, and the violets cover the hills, and turns the white blossoms into black, sweet berries in the autumn? It is your dear and kind Father who does all this for his children. He has very many children; some of them live in houses and some in tents, some in little huts and some under the trees, in the warm countries and in the

The Seven Little Sisters

cold. And he loves them all; they are his children, and they are brothers and sisters. Shall they not love each other?

Made in United States
Troutdale, OR
07/16/2023

11237058R00056